D0514269

The Useless Troll

Written by
Alec Sillifant

Illustrated by
Joëlle Dreidemy

meadowside
CHILDREN'S BOOKS

ONCE UPON A TIME, in a land far, far away, Gretel was skipping happily through The Enchanted Forest.

If you're not sure how to tell if a forest is enchanted, let me explain.

In a normal forest, everything is peaceful and quiet. In an enchanted forest, all the trees talk... endlessly. Usually they are spreading terrible rumours about each other, so... if you're looking for a place to have a quiet picnic... go to a normal forest.

After a full morning of mischief, Gretel was skipping along looking for something else bad to do when she thought she heard a noise above the endless chatter of the trees.

"Quiet!" she shouted and 'quiet' the trees became, for they had no desire to mess with a little girl who had sold her own brother to the not-so-nice Snow White.

Told you it was a sad tale.

With the trees of The Enchanted Forest silenced, Gretel could clearly make out what the noise was.

"I know that sound," smiled Gretel. "Someone is crying."

And she skipped off in the direction of the sobbing.

Soon Gretel came to a clearing in the forest, right in the middle of which was a large troll with his head in his hands.

"What's the matter with him?" asked Gretel of the nearest oak tree.

"I don't know," stammered the ancient tree, frightened that Gretel might carve her name into its side. "But he keeps mumbling something about being useless."

Gretel decided to approach this pitiful creature and sort things out because that was the kind of thing Gretel liked to do…
…in a bad kind of way, of course.

"Coo-ee," called Gretel, cheerfully.

"Go away," sobbed the troll.

"What's the matter?" Gretel asked, moving closer.

"Leave me alone," snapped the troll.

"Maybe I can help," said Gretel. The troll sat bolt upright, bright tears running down his ugly face.

"Help me? No one can help me, I'm useless. I'm the most useless troll in all of troll history!"

"Surely not," smiled Gretel.

"My Dad's a great troll, my Mum's a great troll. Even my little sister is uglier and scarier than me," cried the troll. "I am the most useless troll in my village… in the land… in the world."

s she watched the tears rolling down the troll's face, Gretel had an idea…

…an idea so full of badness it was rotten.

If she could tame a troll she would be really famous and, with him as her pet, she could get up to some of the most wicked things ever imagined. Like the next time the oh-so-pretty Rapunzel let down her hair, Gretel and her troll would be waiting to pull her out of the tower window.

"I don't think you're useless," she said, setting her scheme in motion.

The troll stared
Gretel in the face.
"Not useless!

"What would you know?

"Have you ever been chased from under
a bridge by three goats…?

"Have you ever had children laugh at you
when you try to scare them…?

"Have you ever had fifteen princesses
escape from your castle…?

"Well, have you?"

Gretel had to admit that she hadn't.

"Well I have," sniffed the huge troll.

"I'm useless and everyone knows it."

I don't think you're useless, Mr Troll." The troll sniffed.

"You're just saying that to make me feel better."

"Am not," lied Gretel, crossing her fingers. "I think you're a really, really scary troll."

"I suppose you think I'm ugly too?" snivelled the troll, wiping his runny nose on the back of his huge, hairy hand.

"Hideous, I would say," smiled Gretel.

"Really?" said the troll, smiling to show all of his bent, yellow teeth.

"In fact, I think you are the ugliest, scariest, most evil-looking troll I have ever seen," said Gretel with a nod.

Well, I am one of the biggest trolls around," said the troll, standing up, stretching his huge arms and giving an almighty roar.

"And my breath does smell bad enough to turn milk sour."

"There you go," smiled Gretel, making sure all the nearby trees were watching her success.

"Maybe you're right, little girl. Maybe I can be a great troll like my Dad."

"Sure you can," agreed Gretel.

"Yeah, sure I can!" boomed the troll. "I CAN be bad! I CAN be wicked! I CAN be evil!"

...tasted just
like chicken.

For Mum and Dad
I will always treasure
the grin you gave me
and wear it with pride
A.S

Pour Éric et Lucile,
complices de toujours
et premières victimes de mes
tentatives à dominer le monde!
J.D

First published in 2005
by Meadowside Children's Books
185 Fleet Street, London, EC4A 2HS

Text © Alec Sillifant 2005
Illustrations © Joëlle Dreidemy 2005

The rights of Alec Sillifant and
Joëlle Dreidemy to be identified as the
author and illustrator of this work have been
asserted by them in accordance with the Copyright,
Designs and Patents Act, 1988.

A CIP catalogue record for this book
is available from the British Library.
Printed in U.A.E.

10 9 8 7 6 5 4 3 2 1